Acknowledgements

First, I'd like to thank "God", through which all things are possible. To my kids, I love you guys, and thanks for being my inspiration and motivation.

Special recognition goes to:
Taaj Williams, Samir House, Stacey Bigham, and Latoya Jackson for being supportive without question.

Dear Readers, Thank you!

If this is your first book, or one amongst many. I admire the time and energy you invest into making your child great. Strengthening bonds, communication, vocabulary, and self-esteem are just a few positive effects of reading to your child. I hope by reading this book parents and children find it as fun as it is enlightening.

AS AMYA SLEPT, SHE
AWOKE TO A NOISE;

SOMETHING WAS PLAYING WITH ONE OF HER TOYS.

SHE LOOKED AND SHE LOOKED,
WITH NOTHING IN SIGHT;

So she could see better, Amya turned on the light.

THERE MITTENS THE KITTEN LOOKED UP AND PURRED; "BAD CAT," AMYA SAID, AND RUBBED MITTENS' FUR.

SHE KICKED MITTENS OUT,
AND CLEANED UP THE MESS;

THEN AMYA LAID DOWN
FOR HER BEAUTY REST.

AMYA HEARD HER TOYS
SHAKE, AND THE BOUNCE OF
HER BALL;

AND AS SHE LOOKED DOWN,
GUESS WHAT SHE SAW?

LITTLE GREEN MUNSTERS
WHOSE NOSES WERE RED;

ONE BY ONE RUNNING
BACK UNDER THE BED.

"MOMMY! MOMMY!"
AMYA YELLED LOUD;

BUT WHEN MOMMY CAME,
NO MUNSTERS WERE FOUND.

MOMMY TUCKED AMYA IN, AND KISSED HER GOOD NIGHT;

THE MUNSTERS CAME OUT
AS SOON AS MOM LEFT;

AND THEY PLAYED ALL NIGHT UNTIL THE ROOM WAS A WRECK.

MOMMY LOOKED IN THE ROOM, AND GUESS WHAT SHE SAW...

AMYA, MITTENS, AND THE MUNSTERS ALL ASLEEP ON THE FLOOR.

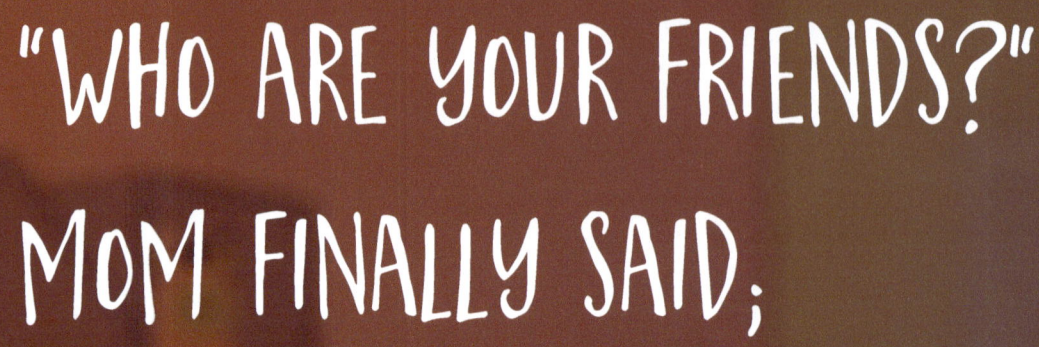

"WHO ARE YOUR FRIENDS?"
MOM FINALLY SAID;

THOSE MUST BE THE MUNSTERS FROM UNDER THE BED.

MUNSTERS
UNDER THE
BED

BY MUTA EL-AMIN

ILLUSTRATED BY DAVID JAMES

 munsters_under_the_bed

 munsters_under_the_bed

MUNSTERS UNDER THE BED. LLC

Art by David James
www.mokojumbiedesign.com

www.ingramcontent.com/pod-product-compliance
Lightning Source LLC
Chambersburg PA
CBHW041544240626
47164CB00002B/124